HILLBILLY HEAVEN

By Bev Beck

Based on a true story!

Mouse Gate Press
1103 Middlecreek
Friendswood, Texas 77546
281-992-3131 TEL
www.MouseGate.com

All rights reserved. Except as permitted under the United States Copyright Act of 1976, No part of this publication may be reproduced, stored in a retrieval system, or transmitted in any form or by any means electronic or mechanical or by photocopying, recording, or otherwise without prior permission of the publisher. Exclusive worldwide content publication/distribution by TotalRecall Publications, Inc.

Copyright © 2020 By: Bev Breece
Cover Art and Illustrations: Bruce Moran

ISBN: 978-1-59095-469-0
UPC: 6-43977-54696-8

FIRST EDITION
1 2 3 4 5 6 7 8 9 10

This is a work of fiction is based on a True Story. The characters, names, events, views, and subject matter of this book are either a product of the author's imagination or are used fictitiously. Any similarity or resemblance to any real people, real situations, or actual events is purely coincidental and not intended to portray any person, place, or event in a false, disparaging, or negative light.

The scanning, uploading and distribution of this book via the Internet or via any other means without the permission of the publisher is illegal and punishable by law. Please purchase only authorized electronic editions, and do not participate in or encourage electronic piracy of copyrighted materials. Your support of the author's rights is appreciated.

This book is dedicated to Josey's family.
May God bless them all!

Authors Bio

Author Bev Beck was born and raised in Missouri. She spent most of her time raising her children in the small town of Owosso, Michigan. She is a domestic engineer and writer of many children's books including, *The Hollers Bunch Goes to Lunch, The Birthday Present, The Acorn Nuts*, with many more to come. She has gathered her inspiration and ideas from her six children and continues to be inspired by her grandchildren.

About the Book

Hillbilly Heaven is based on a true story.

Josey grew up in the bountiful foothills of the Missouri Ozarks with her little brothers and sister.

As her thoughts take her back to those hills, she will make you laugh. The secrets that these beautiful hills hold may startle you.

Josey is a strong-willed youngster that endures a lot of trials. Through memories and secrets, she will reveal to you the tolerance and durability of what children can endure together when left without a choice.

True life can sometimes be more bizarre than any movie!

Chapter 1

What a nice spring day thought Josey, as she sat on her porch swing on Grand Avenue looking at grocery ads.

She had six busy little children. Five beautiful little girls; four brunettes and one with blonde curly hair just like hers. Her one son, who she teased, calling him her favorite son, had to grow up in a house full of ribbons and curls. He didn't seem to mind it too much. He just stayed to himself most of the time.

He kept his room somewhat neat and organized. However, the girls' rooms were always messy. Clothes, hairbrushes, and shoes were everywhere.

Josey's five-bedroom house was a soft apricot dawn, which the store had to specially mix for her. It took her two years to find that color. Pastel house paints were not usually heard of, but she was determined to find just the right shade. Therefore, that is exactly what she did.

The trim was white with lattice beside the windows that were specially cut. There were three big butterflies attached to the front just below the peak of the two-story house. There was a small one-bedroom apartment in the upstairs that Josey rented out.

Rose bushes surrounded the front yard of the house. A wooden half barrel sat in the left-hand corner full of moss roses.

The neighborhood was always full with the bustle of children.

Josey looks up and there whizzing past her split rail fence, was this lively child of five on a baby pink sixteen-inch bicycle. As her peers yell out to her "Angel" she twists and turns around in confusion. Should she go this way or that? She decides that she is going solo, straight ahead. Her soft blonde hair flowing just past her ears leaves the gentle winds in command.

Angel's efforts to conquer the stretch of pavement the previous day show on her right knee and the slightly protruding right side of her forehead, as she rides by. However, the small abrasions on her left hand were achieved today.

The intrusions of these growing battle scars do not seem to lessen the pace of this lively moppet of a mere three feet tall.

Josey notices Angel wearing a green, yellow, and peach v-neck. This mid-length sleeved shirt gives off a rainbow effect in the favorable sunlight. Her short blue jean pinafore swishes up and down as she pedals her beloved bike.

Angel turns into Josey's driveway and dismounts her bike with a leap. The bicycle is left at the fence with a kindly toss.

Angel's bare feet smack the asphalt while up the drive she bounces. A meek, mild voice breaks from her stern, positive look as she speaks.

"Hi can your kids come out to play?" She says with a gentle smile creeping across her cheeks. She waits for a reply. A few freckles sprinkled across the bridge of her nose are vivid as she tilts her head in question.

"Sure Angel, as soon as they finish cleaning their rooms," said Josey.

"Okay," says Angel.

She twirls around on her left foot and bounces forward letting her right foot lead the way back down the driveway.

Angel straddles her bike and thrusts onward with a burst of untamed energy. She tries to master this sudden gust of speed, but falters and crashes into the red Chevette parked at the curb. She amazingly springs from the sunlit pavement with an incredible grin.

This happy child seems to have a wonderful sense of going forward leaving time behind. Angel rides off searching for familiar faces. She looks for approval and gains it while battling for expertise on this two-wheeler. She hollers out "wait for me!" her determination to catch up with the others is quite successful, as this free-spirited child rides out of site.

As she turns her attention back to the grocery store

ads, Josey starts thinking about her family and friends in Missouri where she grew up. The bright sun casts a shadow on the papers as she turned the pages. The wind was blowing just enough to make a perfect day. As she slowly rocked back and forth on her swing, Josey felt a lazy calmness come over her. She peacefully drifted back to her childhood home.

Chapter 2

Josey remembers her first time on a bicycle as not so pleasant. She grew up in the foothills of the Missouri Ozarks with her five brothers and one sister and only one bike.

Her smallest brother Clayton would ride that bike past her whistling like the dickens, which was something she couldn't do either. He was only four years old.

Every time Clayton went past her, she wanted to reach out and knock him off that damn bike. It couldn't be that hard if her little brother almost half her age could do it.

Josey decided she would wait until she was alone to get on that bike and try it again. She just couldn't keep it upright.

After hurting her knees, twisting her left foot, and almost breaking her right thumb; she gave up. She hated that old blue bike. "Who needs to ride a bike in these hills anyway," she screamed out. She couldn't even remember what happened to that stupid thing.

She never rode a bike after that until she was married and had kids, all six of them in fact.

Thinking about that bike took her home again. She

missed Missouri. It was so beautiful, but it held so many secrets. She didn't remember it getting as cold as Michigan, but it must have at times.

The hot sun would beat down on her shoulders, burning the back of her neck as her ponytail would make her sweat from the heat. How she loved that warm mountain air with the grass beneath her feet. The sweet smell of Honeysuckle and Sheepshire would fill the air along the path to school.

Josey's brother Jim was eleven months younger than her. They were the same age for about 3 weeks. Her birthday is in September and his in August. Wayne was younger than Jim, then Ray, Gordon, David, Helen, and then Clayton.

Josey would wander through the tall cool woods near her house just to sit and dream. What will I do when I am on my own? What will my kids look like? How many of them will there be? I know they will all be special. They will be smart and good looking. They will be important people. I will just be married once and stay married forever to one great guy.

The green, gold, and brown thick carpet of leaves would rustle beneath her feet. The towering maples shaded out the hot sun with streaks of light running through their branches.

Josey would sit on a decaying log that had long sense fallen and spend immeasurable amounts of time just being alone. A breezy butterfly would sometimes float by.

How do they live, these tiny animals, in the world we take for granted? The mint green grasshoppers and the crickets as black as coal moved about hastily. The ladybugs would float around without a care.

How do they see this vast Earth of giants big and small?

She could hear her brothers call out to her. "Jo it's time for supper, where are you?" She didn't want to answer. She just wanted to be alone.

How she longed for those wonderful summer days to take her away from this wisdom of torment and age.

She thought of the beautiful Missouri sunrise as it peaked through the foothills in a fiery red and yellow blaze while the rooster sat on a barbed wire fence crowing deep in his throat; his cone straight and tall for all to see. His orange and brown feathers curled to and fro as his loud shrill would break the silence of sleep. The sun was barely up when the chores began. She didn't mind the chores. She liked to keep busy when she was home from school.

School would start in September. It was always on Josey's birthday. It didn't seem quite right, but that's just the way it was.

"Josey, get up for school!" Inez would yell. She would tell Josey to make sure that Helen and the boys were ready for the bus. Josey would get their breakfast and make sure they were clean and their hair was combed. The big yellow bus would come rolling down the hill and they would all run to the end of the driveway to catch it. They all like school. They liked to be with other kids to laugh and play.

Chapter 3

One hot morning, Josey woke up to the rooster uhr...uh.... uhrrring. She pulled the curtains back.

"What the hell?" she hollered. She looked around to make sure that her Aunt Inez did not hear her say hell. She would have gotten a mouthful of soap or worse for sure. She was still half asleep. She had experienced the nasty taste of soap a few times, but she didn't care.

The table in the front yard was covered in blood. A big butcher knife lay on the ground underneath it. Josey ran into the kitchen knocking over a fan that stood near the doorway. Her aunt came out the bedroom in a long raggedy yellow night gown and her red hair in a big fuzzy ball. You could see right through that nightgown but, she liked it and she wore it anyway.

"What is the matter with you," yelled Aunt Inez.

"What happened here?" asked Josey.

"Oh, your Uncle Carl done stole a hog from the neighbors and butchered it last night. You kids clean up the mess and I'll cook you alls breakfast," said Inez.

Josey went to her bedroom where her brother

Clayton and little sister Helen were still sleeping. She sat on the bed still trying to catch her breath. She dressed and then woke her brother and sister. "Hey guys, time to get up! Uncle Carl killed another hog," she told them. "You two go get dressed and I'll start cleaning up the mess," she said. The hot sun shone though the curtains as the two kids got dressed and combed their hair.

Her brothers, Wayne and Jim, went out to milk the cows while Raymond and Gordon went to gather the eggs. Jim didn't like to get the eggs. Last time he did, he reached his hand under the hen and a snake crawled out.

Breakfast was a big pile of bacon, fried eggs, homemade butter, and hot biscuits with cold milk from the milking the day before. The morning had already started out hot and muggy. Opening the door was like opening an oven. Laundry day meant filling the old wringer washer and washtub with buckets from the well. The socks soaked together in a big bucket of bleach water outside.

Josey was in the side yard hanging out a load of sheets when she heard yelling coming from the back of the house where they did the wash. She ran around the side of the house and tripped falling over a small tree branch. "Dammit," she cursed getting up and checking out the cut on her left knee. Limping to the back of the house she screamed, "What is going on? Who's screaming?"

Ray was putting laundry through the wringer when his right hand got caught up in a towel. His arm was pulled into the wringers up to his elbow. He was jumping up and down yelling, "turn off the washer!" He was trying to pull his arm out.

Josey ran behind the washer and pulled the plug from the wall. She had to open the release on the wringers to get his arm out. "Your arm is swollen bigger than shit," she said. She led him to the chair and helped him sit down.

He had to rest it on a pillow with ice to get the swelling down.

"Gotta watch what the hell yer adoin boy," shouted Carl.

Ray was careful with the wringers after that. He got out of doing chores for a few days though. Wayne finished running the towels though the wash and the rinse. Josey hung them on the lines.

"I think the clothes lines are going to have to be moved again Carl," shouted Aunt Inez. "Only this time get them away from the trees. The birds are shittin on the clothes again," she added.

Not again thought Josey. That means they all have to be taken down and washed again. Down came the sheets and back into the wash. Wayne and Jim carried more buckets of water from the well. Only one of the lines had to be rewashed, the one with all the sheets.

Her little brother Gordon was the independent one. At the age of three he would always say, "me go, to bye go." Even then, his heart would wander to unknown places. His spirit wanted to be free. Free to do what? He did not know. Free to go where? He did not care. He wanted to roam.

Wayne's nickname was tubby. Maybe because he was the fattest; you couldn't count "all" of his ribs. He would get nosebleeds and just pass out. Who knew about high blood pressure then?

Helen would hold her breath until she turned blue and passed out. What a scary sight that was!

All of the kids stayed close. They loved each other and looked out for each other. When Helen or Wayne passed out they would all get scared. They would hug and promise to look out for each other; and they did.

Chapter 4

"You kids get yer clothes packed we're amovin back to St. Louis. I got a job at the shoe factory," Aunt Inez yelled as she was going through the house throwing things into boxes.

Josey, Helen, and the boys hated the city.

The streets and sidewalks were sweltering hot in the summer. They had to wear shoes all of the time and stay in the house or fenced in back yard. The yards and some of the streets were made of red brick and the neighbors were too close.

On the weekends Carl and Inez would go out to the bars with Carl's sister and her husband. On Fridays they would come home after work and tell the kids to eat their supper and stay in the house. They could make popcorn, cool aide, and watch the television. They were not to answer the door to anybody. It was always the same thing.

At two in the morning there would be screaming, fighting, and things flying into the walls. Josey and the kids would all huddle under blankets together until it stopped. The next day there were beer cans and broken dishes everywhere. Josey and the boys would sometimes drink the left over beer out of the cans. That was until they started finding cigarette butts in them.

The kids dreaded the weekends. It just seemed like these crazy, scary weekends would never stop. Josey, Helen, and the boys asked their Aunt Inez and Uncle Carl not to go out anymore. But, the long, hot weekends of fighting went on. Josey and the kids decided to get even with them.

One evening, they were all sitting across the couch watching Gilligan's Island. Inez sat in her big chair reading one of her many Perry Mason mysteries. She had them all.

Josey, Helen, and the boys all kept looking at each other grinning. They were trying not to laugh.

Waiting….

Waiting….

Aunt Inez got a funny look on her face. She jumped up and ran into the bathroom. They couldn't hold it in any longer. They all started laughing out loud.

"What's going on in there," shouted Uncle Carl.

Josey rises up and says, "we're wondering when we are getting off this damn island." The boys' eyes got big and they all stopped laughing. "Oh, no," said Jim.

Carl jumped up and stomped into the living room. He looked from one face to the other and said to Josey, "What did you just say?"

"We were just wondering when they are getting off that big island," she said.

"Oh," Carl said, with a weird look. "Well you kids

quiet down." He went back into the bedroom. He was still nursing a hangover.

"That was a close one," whispered Josey. After all, the 'Queen of Kids Not Swearing' was in the bathroom pre-occupied.

Josey got up and went into the kitchen. She slipped the EX-Lax back into the cupboard.

Their Aunt Inez was an avid caffeine hound. Josey and the boys had decided to make her coffee and waite on her that day, more than usual.

"I think it's time we moved back to the country," Carl decided he had enough of the city again for a while. The kids were all happy. The next couple of days were spent getting boxes and packing things.

Carl was looking through the kitchen cupboards one morning while Inez was making a pot of Maxwell house. "Where is the EX-Lax Inez?" he asked.

"It should be in there, I just bought a new box," Inez said.

"This box only has one in it," he says turning around to show her the almost empty box.

"The kids must have gotten into it thinking it was candy," she says smiling, "it serves em right."

For the next few days, she kept tabs on the kids to see who went to the bathroom and when. The only one making frequent trips to the bathroom was her.

Getting even was not easy. One Friday night when Aunt Inez and Uncle Carl were out Josey and the boys decided to fix them both. The screen door in the kitchen would fill with bugs when the porch light was on. The kids gathered lots of the bugs, especially the big pinching June bugs, and put them between the sheets on Aunt Inez and Uncle Carl's bed. They tucked the sheets in tight.

The kids jumped into bed when they heard their aunt and uncle coming up the stairs. They laughed as they heard them tossing and turning while slurring their drunken swear words. The bugs had done the trick.

Chapter 5

Walking though the city dump was hot and dusty. There were piles and piles of stinky old trash bags. On one side of the dump, Josey and the boys would look through the piles of old papers and broken toys. Some things were fixable. Uncle Carl found a couple of old bikes with tires that were blown and brought them home.

He chopped up corn cobs and filled the tires with them. Josey would stand and watch the boys bump up and down the old gravel road on those bikes. They were really bumpy to ride but they worked. Sometimes the corn cobs would rip through the side of the tire but, Uncle Carl would just fix them again. The boys did not mind, they were just happy to have more bikes to ride.

Saturday mornings were bath days, especially after a Friday afternoon visit to the dump. Big pots of water were heated up on the old wood stove. The big metal tub in the side yard was filled with warmed up soapy water. The girls would take a bath first.

The boys had to stay in the back yard. After the girls got done with their bath the boys would take turns, two at a time. There was a blue wash basin on the back porch that was used to wash hands and faces before meals and before school. Their feet were washed in a white wash basin also on the back porch.

There was two big barrels on the side of the house to catch rain water. This was used for washing up, washing hair, and sometimes for washing dishes.

Josey remembered one visit to the dump when Uncle Carl was walking along a ridge where a big hole was dug out and filled with stinky trash. He stepped on a rock and slid sideways down into the hole. He landed in a big pile on nasty garbage.

He was just a cussing. He tried to crawl up the side and back down he went. Josey walked away so he wouldn't see her laughing. That Friday he got his bath early.

On bath day, Josey would tear old pieces of clothes into strips and roll her and Helen's hair up and tie them. Sometimes she would cut an old Prince Albert Tobacco can into strips, cover them with paper, and use them for curlers. They actually worked pretty well. The girls had fluffy, curly hair on Saturday night when they would go to the movies.

While the kids were taking their baths, Inez would make homemade pancakes on old burners on the old wood stove. She made simple syrup with sugar, water, and a little vanilla.

Josey always wanted to make the pancakes. Inez would spit on the old burner lids to see if they were hot enough. Josey would always tell her that she would cook the pancakes so Inez couldn't spit on the stove.

Josey would drop a little water on the burner lids and when they were hot enough, the water would form into little balls that ran around on the lid. The pancake batter was poured by spoonfuls right on the top on that old stove. They were good.

Some of the places they had lived had electricity and some of them didn't. When there was no electricity, or if it got shut off, they would read and do homework by kerosene lamps.

Bedtime was early. Everyone went to bed with the chickens and got up with the roosters.

Josey would lie in the bed and look out the window. She listened to the crickets and the owls. She wouldn't go to sleep until almost daylight. She could hear her brothers snoring and turning over in bed. Clayton and Helen slept in the bed with her. They would fight over who got to sleep next to her so they would take turns. Clayton hardly ever snored, but Helen sure did. Nighttime was very peaceful.

Sometimes Josey would still be awake when the roosters crowed.

Chapter 6

One mid-July a storm hit. Lightening streaked through the sky and thunder cracked. The wind picked up in a rage.

There was a coffee can full of marbles sitting on the kitchen table. That coffee can flew over and the marbles were flying everywhere. Everyone ran for the old cellar in the side yard.

Josey could hear the harsh wind blowing and things flying about. Clayton and Helen huddled with Josey.

The cellar was damp and cool. The dirt smelled sour. The storm didn't last long. It stopped as fast as it started and everything was still again. Carl opened the cellar door. The sun was shining.

Everyone slowly climbed the steps up to the yard. There were a few trees that were broken over. Limbs were everywhere. Josey couldn't hear the birds.

"I wonder if they are okay. How could they be? Where did they go?" she thought.

Heading back to the house Josey saw only two broken windows, one in the kitchen and one in her bedroom in the front of the house. In the kitchen marbles were rolling everywhere. The kids were all picking up dishes, pans, and marbles.

Josey and the boys played lots of marbles. She liked looking at the different kinds. The peewees were small ones. The cat eyes had beautiful different colors. The boulders were the big ones. Most of all Josey loved the cat eye boulders.

The big steel marbles were only used when all the players had one. Josey really didn't like using those. Sometimes they would crack the cat eyes. They were called steelies.

Josey got pretty good at playing marbles and she even made marble bags out of old pieces of sheet. A circle was made in the dirt and each player put the same amount of marbles in the middle of the circle. Turns were taken using a boulder to knock the marbles out of the circle. You got to keep the marbles that you knocked out. Josey gained quite a collection.

She was good at checkers too. She played a lot of checkers with her Uncle Carl. After a time, she was hard to beat.

When her own children were old enough for marbles she made them all marble bags with their names on them. She also taught them how to play.

Josey remembered the old tire swing in the front yard. She liked that swing. It was kinda hard to get into but, it was fun. It was made from an old truck tire and a long thick rope. The kids had to dump the water out of it when it rained.

Climbing inside an old tire and rolling down the hill was fun too. They had fun with a lot of different things. They climbed trees and made tree fortresses with branches.

Josey really liked to climb trees with the boys. She would find a tree that she could go high up from branch to branch and see down all around her. As she watched from one of the branches her brothers came running out of the neighbor's barn. They were laughing and the neighbor was yelling at them. They ran under the tree where Josey was leaning over a big branch.

"Why do they all look green?" she thought as she watched them run home. They had been throwing horse shit at each other in the neighbor's barn. They were covered from head to toe.

Josey got out the soap, a washcloth, and the washtub. They were all soaped up and rinsed. Hair, clothes, and all before their aunt got home that day.

Josey remembered one morning when Wayne went out to milk the cow. It was a cold morning. He started milking the cow and she began to shit everywhere even down her legs. Wayne didn't want to stop to wash her up. He was cold and wanted to just get it done. He was straining all the milk when Uncle Carl came outside. "What the hell are you adoin boy?"

"Straining the milk," said Wayne. There was shit on the bucket and some in the milk. Wayne's hands were also covered in shit. "Throw that damn milk out and get in there to eat," said Uncle Carl.

Just as Wayne went to the pump to wash his hands Uncle Carl yelled, "Oh! No you don't! "You are going to eat just like you are shit and all."

Wayne had to eat with his shitty hands. No fork. No spoon. Just his hands, that was a lesson well learned.

Chapter 7

"It's your turn to be it," Ray called out.

Josey looked out the big window in front of the house. The boys were playing hide and seek. It was Butch's turn to be it. It was still daylight out. Butch hid his face against the tree. All the boys ran and hid except Wayne. He jumped up on a nearby fence post and just stood there.

Butch yells, "ready or not here I come!" He was running around the yard finding boys one by one. He couldn't find Wayne who was standing right in plain sight on that fence post right above where they were playing. All the boys even started to help Butch look for Wayne. They were all walking around that fence and never looked up. Josey couldn't believe it. It was the funniest thing that she ever saw. They never did find him until he jumped down right in the middle of them. "What silly boys," thought Josey.

When their cousins would come over, they played hide and seek until after dark. Sometimes they would even go in the house and sit in a row on the floor playing I-spy. One kid would name a color and the others would have to guess what the object was that they described. Josey remembered playing all these games. They were happy with these things.

Her children didn't have a lot, but the girls had dolls and her son Billy had an Atari video game. She encouraged them to play outside with their marbles, jump rope, and things that they could share.

They chased fireflies at night and they love playing in the rain. They had bikes and plenty of friends down the street to play with. They played hide and seek with the other kids until dark sometimes too.

Josey would watch them play and remember her own childhood. She taught them how to play checkers. She had a sandbox built for them in the back yard. Her play yard was dirt and mud but that was ok too. She didn't know about sandboxes back then.

Josey, her brothers, and Helen did often play in the rain as long as there was no lightening. One evening during a storm, all the boys went out to pee off the porch before going to bed. Lightening hit the post right next to Ray.

The boys all screamed and ran in the house pushing and shouting to get in the door. That sure scared the hell out of those boys.

Chapter 8

One Thanksgiving Uncle Carl brought home the biggest turkey Josey had ever seen. She helped clean and stuff it. Good corn bread stuffing with lots of onions was great. The homemade apple pies were wonderful.

Josey's Aunt Inez would make huge yeast biscuits that you could smell baking, even outside. There were also canned berries and peaches.

Josey couldn't wait until dinner was ready. The big turkey baked for hours in the low oven of the old wood stove.

While dinner was cooking, Josey, Helen, and the boys cleaned the house. They washed the walls, swept and mopped the floors, and thoroughly cleaned the bedrooms. They even cleaned and mopped the porch, and swept out the outhouse.

The turkey was a delicious golden brown. Inez made a big bowl of turkey gravy while Josey peeled potatoes. There were lots of mashed potatoes and the green beans sizzled in a big skillet with bacon. There was homemade butter for the biscuits and cold, fresh cow's milk to drink.

When dinner was ready, everyone sat at a huge

table and Grace was said.

After dinner the kids had done the dishes in a big pan on the table. When everything was put away, the television was turned on.

Josey and little Helen were stretched out on the couch. The boys were all on the floor. There was an old black and white movie on. Clayton looked up and said, "I have to go to the bathroom."

He jumped up and ran out the door, slamming the old screen. "What hit him," Josey thought. He was sure in a hurry.

To go to the outhouse at night was not fun, especially in the cold. It was set back a ways behind the house near the woods.

Next Ray had to go. Then Gordon and Jim had to go. They nearly knocked each other over going through the door.

Josey thought it was odd that all of a sudden everyone had to go. It was a race to the outhouse. It looked like everyone was all of a sudden running in fast motion.

Uncle Carl tried to take a short cut by the side of the house to beat Josey there. However, he forgot that the cloths line was moved there and it hung low as the kids did the wash.

Running between the two trees, taking that short cut he got his neck caught on that line and down he went. Needless to say he didn't make it to the outhouse. That was a memorable Thanksgiving in deed. That big turkey got its revenge on them for several days. That was the last Thanksgiving that there was a wild turkey served.

In the late fifties and early sixties times were very different. Christmas came and went without much thought about gifts. The kids really didn't miss much and life seemed okay the way it was. They didn't know any different they just played amongst themselves.

Summer outdoors with each other was fun. They didn't need toys, nature was enough. Heck, having each other was enough. Sticks, rocks, and mud pies occupied their time. The daily chores, work around the yard, and in the fields kept them busy and tired.

Chapter 9

Josey and Ray were in the front yard one cool afternoon playing Ray's favorite thing, soldiers.

They were sword fighting with a couple of plastic bleach bottles. Josey tripped over a tree branch and just as she started to fall Ray swung his bottle. WHAM! It hit Josey right in her left eye. It sent her for a loop. She fell to the ground and sat with her head down. She couldn't see for a few minutes. When she looked up Ray said, "Oh my GOSH!" her eye had swollen up. She went into the house and put a cold towel on it. She told Inez she tripped over a rock and fell on a branch.

The next morning her eye was big and black. She told the kids at school that she got into a fight and won. "Who cares what they think anyway?" she thought.

Some brands of bleach came in brown glass bottles. Helen was playing with one of those old brown bottles a few months before that and fell on it. Three of her little fingers were nearly cut off. They were cleaned and had to be wrapped in gauze for a really long time. They finally healed with some Watkins salve. That salve was used for everything. It did always seem to work. They had the green cloverleaf salve and the brown salve in the kitchen cupboard all the time, right next to the ex-lax and the castor oil. The kids all got a spoonful of old castor oil once in a while whether they needed it or not.

They stood in line and cried when they had to take it. It was like eating a spoonful of grease. Of course they didn't have to take it around turkey time.

While walking to the road to get the mail one hot afternoon, Josey stepped on a piece of glass. She cut her foot about two inches wide; she wrapped it up with a piece of an old shirt. It was in the arch of her right foot and it hurt her to walk. It soon got infected.

Josey soaked it in warm salt water and kept clean wraps on it until it healed up. Even with the many cuts and stone bruises on her feet she hated shoes.

She only wore them when she had to, like going to school or going to town. She had small feet. She could wear her little brother Clayton's shoes and sometimes she did.

One Valentine's Day she wore his shoes to school. When she got to school she noticed that the front of the sole on the left shoe had come loose. Every time she would take a step the sole of the shoe would slap on the floor. Her class was having their Valentine party and they all pushed the chairs into a circle. The teacher would call a name to get a Valentine that was addressed to them. Every time she called Josey's name her shoe would slap the floor as she walked up to get it.

What a pain in the ass that was. Not to mention the laughs but, Josey didn't care. She soon learned how to glue shoes. She would use card board to put inside them too. She didn't care, she didn't like shoes anyway.

Most of the time kids all wore high top shoes. There were snakes in the woods and around the yard. Once there was a snake in the kitchen drawer. When her Aunt Inez opened it to get out a dish towel she let out a scream that could have woke the dead. "Get this damn snake out of the house Carl," she screamed.

He came out of the bedroom laughing so hard he hit his head on the open cupboard next to the door. He was laughing and coughing so hard that Inez got mad and threw a knife at him. He ducked and just kept laughing. He pulled the snake out of the drawer and threw it outside. He laughed all the way back to the bedroom. Inez was mad and was still throwing things around the kitchen. The next morning Carl fixed the screen door so that it would shut tight so no more snakes could get in.

Chapter 10

In the little school house, there were two classes in each room. The teacher would walk to one side and give an assignment to one grade. Then she would go to the other side and give the other grade a spelling test or something.

It was a cozy little school. Josey made a few friends. She loved softball games between the local schools. Josey loved softball. That is until she got smacked in the knee with a bat. A boy that was on her team, that she liked, threw the bat after hitting the ball. She didn't like him much after that. She didn't really even play ball much after that, at least for a while. Then, her favorite thing was watching the old black and white television.

One evening while watching Gilligan's Island, Josey heard a big commotion in the dining room. "Jim went out last he was supposed to shut it," said Wayne.

"No, Ray was out last," said Jim.

"Well, one a you boys is a lyin and somebody better tell the truth," shouted Uncle Carl.

Josey could hear the boys crying out as the belt flew with a slap from one boy to the other. Wayne cried out as the old razor strap cracked across his back. It seemed the boys had left the gate to the chicken coop open and the chickens were running everywhere. There were Rhode Island Reds, Japanese Silkies, big white hens, and several roosters all running down the driveway.

Josey hated to hear her brothers crying. She had to experience that damn razor strap a few times herself.

Once her and Jim were wresting in the house and knocked the radio off the counter. Here comes their uncle with that strap, "which one knocked over the radio?"

Jo and Jim just stood and looked at each other. Who Knew? They were both playing around. The welts on their legs lasted for days. Josey had forgotten about that, or at least thought she did.

Another Saturday afternoon Josey and Jim were playing around slapping each other with sticks. Jim accidently hit her across the face as she turned. She yelled out, "You bitch!"

Here comes Aunt Inez out the door. Josey quickly said, "stop it you Butch! Don't hit me in the face you Butch."

Their aunt stood there for a moment just looking at the two of them. She wasn't quite sure what she heard. After a thoughtful look back and forth at them, she decided Butch is what she heard. Jim held the nickname Butch from then on.

Their Aunt Inez could hear a mile away. It was a good thing she didn't hear too clear that day. She used more cuss words than Josey knew was invented. Kids just were not allowed to say them.

The next day the principal and the bus driver came to talk to Inez and Carl about changing the bus routes. They were standing in the front yard talking and here comes one of the milk cows around the house. That old cow walked right up to the bus driver, looked him straight in the eye, turned around, and started peeing.

The bus driver, whatever his name was, jumped back and slipped on a big flat rock laying behind him. He nearly lost his foothold.

Carl started laughing and coughing on his cigar. The principal, whatever his name was, said "I guess we better get going." The bus driver was slapping at the side of his pants, wet with mud and the cow's generous spray.

When they drove off Inez put her hands on her hips and yelled at Carl. "That ain't funny Carl. Now that bus driver might not pick up these kids for school. Why ain't that damn cow tied up anyway? You kids get that damn cow around back and tie it up."

The bus driver did show up the next morning. He didn't say a word but, he still looked mad. Josey, Helen, and the boys made it a point to be good and quiet riding that bus, at least for the next month or so.

Josey liked riding the school bus. She would sit near a window and look out. She kept to herself most of the time. It wasn't because she didn't like people, she really did. She just didn't want to talk. She liked sitting alone and being alone with her own thoughts. She just wanted to daydream and imagine what another life would be like. She didn't want to be without her sister and brothers but, she would surely take them all with her, even in her daydreams.

Chapter 11

Josey remembered one night when the boys wouldn't go to sleep. She could hear them arguing.

"What in the hell is going on in there? You boys better quiet down," they woke up Uncle Carl. "Here we go again," she thought.

Josey heard him jump out of bed and stomp into the boys' room.

"They won't quit letting stinks," said Ray.

Out came the razor strap. "You boys knock that shit off, you better go to sleep," shouted Uncle Carl. "I'll bring in my belt and it'll be harder next time," he added stomping back to his room. He cracked his foot on the way and yelled, "Owwwwhhhh, damn you boys. You all better get to sleep."

Uncle Carl got up the next morning to a dirty kitchen. Inez had left for work, where ever that was. "You mean you kids didn't do the dishes last night?" He said.

He had beer cans lying all over the house from the day before. "You kids get this shit cleaned up and put the beans away, that's what you're having for supper," he added.

Josey will never forget the taste of sour bean soup.

Sometimes they would have what Inez called Kenedi meat. You couldn't tell what it was but, it tasted alright. Josey didn't know if it was pork or beef or something else but, it wasn't chicken. She just knew it came in a can and it was free. They baked it, boiled it, fried it, and sometimes it was even put in soup.

Josey even made what she called baked soup. It had potatoes, onions, garlic, sometimes carrots, Kenedi meat, lots of water, and she would put it in the oven.

When the chickens were plenty, Uncle Carl would pull the heads off a couple of them and Inez would fry them. That woman could cook a good meal thought Josey. She could make something out of nothing.

Josey loved her chocolate gravy over hot biscuits with fresh cow's milk. The cream on the top was an inch thick.

In the morning Josey would sit with a jar of milk that was kept out overnight. She would sit in the old rocker and shake it up. The next morning they would have fresh butter and buttermilk. The kids all helped work in the garden.

Josey would slip a salt shaker into her pocket and go out to sit in the rows of tomatoes. They were so warm and good right off the vine. She would wash the tomatoes and peel them for canning, eating them while she worked.

There were green beans, peas, corn, melons, lettuce, and cucumbers. Josey loved fried green tomatoes.

There was fresh meat, home grown vegetables, and fresh cow's milk. Josey also looked forward to Aunt Inez's chocolate mayonnaise cake. Who could ask for more?

Chapter 12

Josey headed back to the woods for more peace, but it was not so quiet this time. The birds seemed to be chirping really loud that day. She thought about how such little things could be so loud.

Sitting on her log she looked down and sees a dead bird. She picked it up and began to cry. She looked at the little mouth and feet.

It's red feathers were beautiful. "I wonder what happened," she thought. She wanted to know what this tiny little animal was made out of. She put the little bird in a knot hole in the log. The next time she came to the woods she brought a small, sharp kitchen knife.

She cut the little bird open to see the insides. She was surprised to see that it was much like a chicken. The tiny little neck and throat was very small. How could it be that they could sing so loud? God was a genius. She buried that bird close to her log. Then she sat and wondered if she would ever leave Missouri.

She always wanted to know about other people and different places. Since Missouri borders eight states surely she would get to see one of them someday or maybe she would just live in the boot heel forever. Even though it was the lowest and flattest of the Ozark foothills and the poorest part of the state, it was her home.

The area just north of the state was rolling hills and fertile plains. The Missouri River flows from the northwest to the southwest. However, the Mississippi River runs alongside the state right next to St. Louis.

Josey spent a lot of time learning about her state. Even though she had it in her heart that she would travel someday she loved Missouri and wanted to know more about it. Josey just knew her Aunt and Uncle would be happy that she learned Missouri was the leading alcohol and tobacco state. They sure got their fair share.

Central Missouri was also known for its cotton. Cotton was the longest running crop and the harvesting could last well into November. It would start out being a pretty plant with white flowers. She always thought it was strange when she saw the flowers turn pink then red. She really liked them when they were pink.

The pretty red flowers would fall off then green pods would appear. This was the boll that would open up into the fluffy white cotton. The cotton would get spun into cloth. She also remembers watching the seeds get crushed and she learned that this was used to make oils and shortenings. The part that confused Josey was that if they crushed the seeds, what did they use to grow more?

They also used the lint on the seeds to make plastic explosives and paper. She thought about how much time that must take to get that part off. It must have taken an awful amount of seeds too.

Josey knew that cotton came in white, brown, and green. For a time color was put into the plants making them different colors. "How the heck did that work?" She wondered.

Josey was thinking back to the cotton picking vacations from school. The kids would work in the fields. Josey thought the cotton fields were welcoming. No one yelled and no one talked. Everyone just worked, even the youngest ones. They would pick the cotton and put them into homemade tow-sacks.

They were made out of flour sacks or potato sacks. They had straps for the shoulder and were drug along behind to be filled. Every now and then a snake would slither across the rows.

At noon they would sit on the sacks of cotton and have a bologna sandwich with a glass of cool-aide or lemonade.

If Josey and the boys worked hard enough all week, on Saturday they would get a quarter to go to the movies. They would also get a dime for a coke. They looked forward to that.

Sometimes little Helen and Clayton would get to go too if Josey looked after them. The Elvis movies were the best. Josey liked to hear all the new Elvis songs.

Working in the fields all week long was worth it.

The long white rows seemed never ending in the hot sun. The soft white cotton seemed weightless, but somehow they managed to get a lot of cotton in a day. The bolls would tear into their fingers, but they learned really quickly to pull that cotton out of the bolls without cutting their hands.

Josey remembered that there were a couple pickings from the fields. The bolls were green and opened at different times then there was more for the second or third round.

When the cotton was just about done for the season, the bolls were picked and the cotton was all extracted from them by machines. You had to wear gloves for that, sometimes the bolls were razor sharp.

Then Josey's mind thought back to Aunt Inez yelling, "Which one of you damn kids shit in my cotton row? I drug my sack in it." She was steaming mad.

She turned her sack over and there was a big pile that ran all down the whole bottom side of it.

Clayton looked up at Josey and grinned. She certainly wasn't going to tell. Carl started laughing and choking on his cigar smoke. The fight was on.

"You think it's so damn funny you can carry the shitty sack up to the scales and weigh it and empty it," shouted Inez.

"You can carry your own damn shitty sack," Carl yelled back.

"Which one of you kids did that?" She yelled, looking around but every kid had their head down working to beat the band. Uncle Carl said still laughing, "It was probably the one that likes to eat the EX-Lax."

Needless to say, everyone went home early that day. That didn't happen too often. Eventually machines were used to pick all the cotton.

Josey actually missed the cotton fields. She remembered bending down in the rows in the hot sun and sometimes got down on her knees when the rows of plants were short. Josey liked to work. When she worked life was peaceful.

Chapter 13

One hot afternoon Josey was sitting in the garden eating tomatoes watching Ray play soldier. He came marching around the side of the house. He had a piece of a tree limb over his shoulder doing some serious singing and marching. He didn't know he was actually headed into battle.

"I'm in the army now. I'm in the army now. Sam, Sam, gosh damn, I'm in the army now. I'll never get rich digging this ditch, you son-of-a-bitch. I'm in the army now. Sam, Sam, gosh…."

Just at that moment the long arm of the law, Colonel Cussword herself, threw her arm out the window just like a retracting rubber band and slapped Ray to the ground. Her arm stretched out a few extra feet it seems.

Well, here she came out the door to throw Private Raymond into the brig. He spent the next hour smelling wallpaper. Talk about battle scars. Josey wondered if he still has them. Ray very seldom got into trouble. He was most of all honest. He wouldn't tell a lie if you asked him to.

For such a God fearing boy he seemed to get hurt a lot. Close to winter Uncle Carl built an ox cart. The kids would haul logs from the woods across the muddy fields. Carl would chop it then; they would bring it home and stack it for the old wood stove. The kids would split some of the logs up with an old ax.

One cold night, Ray was stoking the fire to add more wood and a big hot cinder popped out. It went right down into the side of his boot. He jumped around the house screaming. He finally got his boot off but, he burnt the skin right off his ankle.

Wasn't long after that, Ray was sitting in a chair next to the stove and the chair fell over. He was pinned up against the stove and couldn't get up. It burnt his whole side. Thank goodness for the Watkins's brown salve.

Most of the time Ray was a happy go lucky kid. He liked to laugh and joke around with everyone. When the big sow had piglets, Ray had to sleep in the barn with them. He had to make sure that the sow didn't lay on one of her babies. It never failed, every time that sow had babies, Ray would be right there to sleep.

It was Josey's job to feed the pigs. Clayton would walk through the pig pen carrying an empty bucket calling them while she jumped in the pin, dumped the slop in the trough, and jumped back out real fast. When the pigs heard the slop hit the trough they would turn around and run for it. If he wasn't fast they would knock him right down.

Of course, Ray wasn't the only one that got hurt.

The kids were not allowed to have anything to drink after six o clock. Josey remembers one evening when little Clayton was crying and hiccupping really bad. He had drunk some kerosene from a jar. He had to be rushed to the hospital and get his stomach pumped. He was very sick for a few days but, he luckily survived.

One afternoon, Clayton came running down the path from the road with the mail. "Hey we got another dunn," he shouted.

Uncle Carl ran out of the house and smacked him across the face. Don't be yelling that so the neighbors can hear. Clayton knew that a dunn was special mail. He didn't know at the time that they were bills. He wondered how, could the neighbors hear that. The houses were not that close.

Josey kept thinking back.

The sun was hot and she felt dizzy. She never let her mind think about all of this before but, the memories kept coming.

Chapter 14

It was Christmas time and snow was flying. They didn't usually get much but they didn't care. This year Aunt Inez told them things were going to be different. She went to the little store down town and asked for credit. The boys got cowboy hats and guns. Clayton got one of those silly stick ponies. He drove everyone crazy running around the house with it. Josey got a new purse with pictures of Sal Mineo on the front. Helen got a nice doll. They moved away the next week. The bill was never paid. "How could they do that?" thought Josey.

The house that they moved into leaned to the right really bad. Everyone stood outside in the front yard looking at the house. It made you kind of want to lean with it. Inside didn't seem so bad. The pump was standing in the middle of the kitchen floor. At least the kids did not have to go outside for water. They were all cheering up and down about that.

There was a toilet in the middle of the front room. No more outhouses with the little half moon on the door. I guess the half moon was for air, though it really didn't seem to help much. Now they had a toilet in the house, but Uncle Carl had to build walls around it.

They took turns flushing it just to see it work.

This made Josey remember the outhouse they had years before. It was double seated and had a long crack in it from one seat to the other. You had to be careful because, it would pinch your ass and that was very irritating. Josey thought many times about fixing it but, didn't quite know how.

After moving to the new house, Aunt Inez and Uncle Carl had decided that they were going to quit drinking. Inez was ready to start going to church. The old tent revivals started. Josey, Helen, and the boys all went with her. Carl wouldn't go to church. Aunt Inez couldn't get Carl to go into a store. He was not sociable at all.

When he drove her anywhere, he would sit in the car and wait for her. he didn't like people at all.

Aunt Inez stopped smoking, drinking, and even swearing. That time frame was like being in a twilight zone. She didn't even look the same. She teased and played with the kids. She even hugged them all a lot. The fights with her and Uncle Carl stopped. Those were some of the good times. The world was right and the kids were happy. Uncle Carl would even smile now and then.

One night at the revival a lady came running down between the rows of seats towards Josey. She got down on one knee and said, "Josey why don't you come and get saved?" Josey kept telling the lady that she didn't want to right then. All she remembered was this lady's knee being down in the dirt and she was about ready to pee in her pants. She just wanted this lady to leave her alone.

As soon as the lady got up and left, Josey ran out the side of the tent. She looked around and no one was in sight. She squatted and did what she had to do.

Josey saw shadows moving from behind that big tent, she decided to see who was there. She wished she had never gone back there.

It was Aunt Inez and the preacher. They were kissing and moving about. Oh no, Josey thought. This isn't right after all she is married to Uncle Carl. The preacher must have been giving her lessons on what not to do.

It didn't take long for Uncle Carl to get wise to his wife's fascination with the preacher man. One night they fought about it. He called her a Bible toting infidel. The drinking, cussing, and fighting all started again.

Well, back to reality!

Chapter 15

While sitting in the garden one afternoon pouring salt on a big, red tomato, Josey started thinking about God. What did he look like, and how come she never heard about a Mrs. God? Where was she in all of this?

As she bit her warm tomato she thought about all of the people in the world. How did God do such a fantastic job of making millions and millions of people so different? Everyone she had seen was different. Everyone's face must be about ten inches by ten inches. How could he take that many people and such a small space to work with and make them all different? The only people who looked alike were twins and there weren't that many of them that she knew of.

What about babies? Their faces were even smaller. She thought that some babies did look kind of alike but not that much. Of course everybody's hair was also different. But there were only blondes, brunettes, and redheads. "That cannot account for too much difference," Josey thought.

Josey remembered hearing a conversation between her little sister Helen and a boy that her Aunt Inez babysat for a short time. It was about how babies were born. The little boy said "my mommy told me that babies come out of where you pee." Helen gave him a funny look and said, "no they don't they come from out of the mom's bellybutton."

Josey thought that her little sister was so smart and obviously right. What other explanation could there be? She did not really want to think about that much.

Josey liked to learn on her own but she hated being in school and she thought that history was a good subject. History is where she learned more about other states and other types of people. She liked to learn to add and how to write. But what she really wanted to learn more about was life.

How did little birds fly but, chickens couldn't? She only really saw the chickens fly about two feet as they were coming out of the hen house but that was it. Also, what changed the weather too? It changes from being hot and sunny to being very cold.

All of the vegetables grew out of the ground but, came up different. Of course, you did have different seeds but, how did the first seed ever get started? All of the deep thinking made Josey very tired. She finished her tomato then laid down in the rows and went to sleep in the hot sun.

When she woke up her face, arms, and legs were sunburned. After that she decided that she was never going to fall asleep in the garden again. However, she would still find a place to nap under shade trees.

One time after napping under a nice smelling pine tree, she woke up with her feet and legs all itchy. She had fallen asleep in a bed of poison oak. Poison ivy didn't bother her much but, poison oak sure did. She had to take baths in baking soda water for several days. Needless to say she was more careful about where she napped after that but, sleeping outside was always more peaceful than sleeping in the house.

She would lie on the little porch to look at the stars and one time a ladybug had landed on her arm. In the dim night she watched it move slowly down her arm, its wings came out, and it flew off. Ladybugs did fly but, not very far or high. They have very tiny wings. Josey liked looking for the different colored bugs.

Chapter 16

When Josey would sleep on the porch the thought of snakes didn't much bother her. Her little sister snored something awful. How could such a big sound come from that little mouth. She loved her little sister but she was annoying.

Being out in the country there was mostly just family. Josey sometimes wanted someone her own age to talk to. During school days she really did not talk much to the other girls. They had better clothes and thought they were better than her. She did make a couple of friends like Linda and Susie.

Susie was the shy, quiet type and Linda was all full of fun and pranks. They were all Josey really needed. Sue was a friend to sit with, talk with, bake cookies with and learn dance moves with. However, Linda was very different. Now and then, Josey would find herself getting into a little trouble when she was with Linda.

One morning in school they decided that they were bored and it was time to do something about those snotty girls who always looked down on them. Josey and Linda asked to be excused to use the restroom. Josey took one restroom and Linda took the other.

They locked all the stall doors, crawling out underneath them as they were locked.

When the bell rang Josey and Linda stood back and watched the girls try to get into the stalls. Some of them panicked and ran to the principal's office. Josey and Linda went into the library laughing. The next day they were called into the principal's office.

The principal said "Do you girls know anything about the restroom stalls getting locked yesterday?" "No," said Josey. "We don't know who did it," said Linda.

Well one of the girls said that you two called her pissy pants. "No we didn't, we just called her prissy pants because she was rude to us," said Josey.

"Okay then, go back to your classroom and behave yourself," said the principal. They ran down the hall holding hands and laughing. No one really ever found out who did it.

In the summer, she missed her two best friends. She lost track of Linda through the years but, she stayed in touch with Susie. Susie always stuck up for her no matter what happened. She always believed in her. Years later Susie even became her sister-in-law.

Josey just kept thinking more and more about her schooldays.

After school her Uncle Carl would sit the kids down and teach them math. He knew his times table very well. They sat night after night learning the numbers, one times one clean up to nine times nine. Josey thought that Uncle Carl was pretty smart. She didn't know until years later that he could not read.

Chapter 17

One day walking down the school hall, Josey's skirt started slipping down on the right side. It was given to her by someone at the school office. She did not know who. She was called to the principal's office and was given a big box of clothes.

She liked the skirt but, it was too big. She just rolled the waistband up about four folds and that seemed to do the trick. A couple of girls were walking behind her and started laughing. She ran into the bathroom and rolled that skirt back up. She decided that it was time to learn how to sew. She sat in her bedroom and worked on the clothes. She did make a few errors but kept working until she got it right.

She took a pair of scissors and cut the skirt down the side taking off the waistband. She took out the zipper and cut off about two inches on each side. Then she sewed the zipper back in just to realize that she sewed it in upside down. She held that skirt up and said, "Are you kidding me? How the hell did I do that?" Out came that zipper and she started over. Once the zipper was in right and the skirt was sewn up at the waistband she found that she had sewn that waistband to the skirt she was wearing.

Needless to say she had to cut those stitches out and start over. She finally got that skirt back together and held it out. She thought it looked pretty good. "But now I need to hem it," she said. She cut about four inches from the bottom as well, turned it under about two inches, and put a nice hem in it.

The skirt fit good and looked good. Josey quickly became a self taught seamstress. She just kept learning as she went. It actually came by her naturally. Her aunts and her mother all sewed. One of her aunts worked in a factory making little Brownie dresses and her grandmother worked at a garment factory making different clothes.

Through the years Josey learned to quilt, make dolls, clothes, pillows, and pretty much anything that she could with materials that she had. Josey learned to make do with what she had. If there was something to do she would find a way to get it done.

She helped fix the windows in the house. She painted, laid linoleum, and carpet. She worked on the roof of the chicken coup and on the fences. If something didn't go right she would undo it and start over. Whatever she did it had to be just right.

She even sewed her sister and brothers' clothes. Her hands endured many needle sticks as she learned. However, she quickly learned not to do that so much.

One cloudy school morning Josey was getting dressed. Her uncle came in her bedroom and slapped her in the face with a pair of jeans. "Fix these," he said. The zipper left a mark across the right side of her face.

Inez came in and said "what happened to your face?" Josey told her that she scratched it on the fence. Inez looked at her then turned and walked out. There was no fence.

That next morning was a Saturday. Inez had to work overtime that day. Carl sent the boys and Helen outside. He told Josey that she had to sweep the house. While she was sweeping the kitchen Carl called her into the bedroom. He was lying on the bed naked and his Willie stood straight up.

She kept her head down and walked sideways around the room with the big straw broom trying not to see him. She was shaking and wondering what he was going to do.

"Sweep this room," he said. Josey started to cry. "Sweep under the bed too," Carl said. She started sobbing and shaking even worse. He laughed at her like a villain. She dropped the broom and turned her back on him covering her eyes crying even harder now.

He picked up a shoe beside the bed and threw it at her. It hit her in the back. "Get out of here," he shouted. She ran out the door slamming the screen. Helen and the boys ran up to her. They asked her what was wrong as they all hugged her. She told them that she hit her head on the kitchen cupboard.

As she sat on the ground Clayton rubbed the top of

her head and said, "does that feel better?" "It sure does," Josey said.

They all sat down in the dirt with her. They sat quietly together for a while as if they all knew something was wrong. They sat there just looking at each other until Inez came home and they had to wash for supper.

Chapter 18

In the hot summer, Uncle Carl would take the kids swimming at Cane Creek. One afternoon he decided to take them all to the swimming hole behind an old brick school house. The swimming hole that lay at the far left of this once busy school yard was still a great spot to gather and beat the country heat. The bottom of the secluded water hole was embedded with slippery smooth rocks. The water was cool and clear.

Homemade lemonade was a real treat. The rind halves would float around the big glass jar mixing with the sugar crystals and the seeds lining the bottom. It was satisfying when the family all got together on Saturday afternoons and went swimming. Reality would set in on the number of cousins that there actually were.

This wonderful place was shaken one day when Ray nearly drowned. Carl just barely heard the cry for help. Ray was gulping and struggling, trying hard to get back to his tolerable level of water. However, the slippery rock bottom left him helpless.

As Josey looked up and heard the weak cries, she felt her heart stop beating. Her face turned cold.

Uncle Carl finally got a grip on the defying rocks

and pulled her brother to safety. They went back to swimming at Cane Creek after that. That day was one of the few good memories Josey had of her Uncle Carl and Aunt Inez.

They did not have to take care of her, Helen, and the boys but, they did.

They were uneducated and had done the best they knew how.

They had one daughter, Sandy. Sandy was not around much. She was older and was gone a lot. Sometimes she would take Josey to town with her. Sandy would meet her friends at the sugar shack for malts. They would dance to the juke box. They had long poodle skirts with black and white saddle shoes. The sweaters had their initials on them. They wore scarves tied around their necks and their hair was in ponytails. The can-can slips would show as they bopped around the room. Josey liked going with Sandy and getting out of the house. It did not happen very often.

Josey remembered missing the bus one September morning. Carl came in and asked her, "Why aren't you in school? What are you doing here?"

"I missed the bus," she said.

In what seemed like slow motion, he walked around the table with a wild look on his face. A slight grin came across his mouth. Josey knew something was very wrong. This didn't look like her Uncle Carl anymore. This was something creepy like she had seen on television. What was he doing, she thought? This truly could not be happening. She never noticed how huge his hands were before. He looked like a big grizzly bear, reaching out for his prey.

As he got closer his breath blew across her face. Josey turned and picked up a melon knife from the counter. She slashed the giant hand that was coming at her.

Carl looked down at his hand then he looked back up at her. The grin on his face slowly turned to anger. Josey dropped the knife and ran out slamming the screen door behind her. She ran into the woods beside the house.

"He's going to kill me," she breathed. Her heart was pounding hard in her chest. She sat on the log trying to catch her breath. She sat there with her legs frozen around the log. She knew she eventually had to go home. She sat still listening for footsteps.

She was sure he would be coming after her.

She could hear birds and squirrels rustling about. She could finally breath again but, she waited and waited.

How could he do this to her? What was he going to do anyway? Whatever, it was it had to be bad to scare her so badly.

"Oh my God, I cut his hand with that knife," she cried. She knew she had to go home eventually. What else was she going to do?

She sat alone and the woods seemed to slowly surround her. For a moment she felt as though she was going to pass out. She took slow deep breaths. I'll have to wait until the other kids get home, she thought.

She waited.

She finally heard the others coming down the driveway. She slowly walked to the edge of the woods and waited until they got close to the house. She walked out behind them.

"Jo, what are you doing?" said Butch.

"I missed the bus," said Josey.

"We know" said Butch.

"I was just taking a walk waiting for you guys to come home so I could walk to the house with you all," Josey said.

Josey avoided looking her uncle in the face. She never realized how big and strong he was before.

At the dinner table he would look down at the cut on his hand and then look at Josey with a, you've had it, look. He had cut his hands many times working on the combine machine. After a long day of working in the soy bean fields another cut on his hand could go unnoticed.

Thinking about that day reminded Josey of some of the other memories she had thought she forgotten about.

Knowing now what she didn't know back then

made those memories even more terrifying. She wished things would have been different. She wanted life to be so much better and kinder for her own children. She wondered if time healed those memories for her sisters and brothers, whom she loved so much. Even though they lived far apart now, they kept in touch and kept as close as they could.

Chapter 19

It was time to pack again. They moved many times and there they were back to the outhouses.

Josey tried to stay close to her brothers and little sister. She would try to keep everyone even herself away from her uncle's glares.

How she wished they would go back to the city where Carl was gone most of the time. He worked in a factory and Aunt Inez worked at the shoe factory. Josey and the kids were alone a lot. As long as they were fighting, they were ignoring the kids.

While working in the garden one evening, Josey looked up and didn't see her little sister Helen anywhere. She ran into the house. Helen was not there. She called for her, "Helen, where are you?"

She heard her scream from out behind the house. The outhouse door flew open and Carl was laughing a loud obnoxious laugh. As he shoved Helen to the ground, he walked off into the soy bean field. Josey ran to help her little sister up.

"What did he do to you?" asked Josey, but Helen wouldn't say anything. She just kept crying.

Josey did not make anymore quiet trips into the woods. She watched over her younger siblings even more after that. Another drunken weekend of fighting was coming for sure.

The drinking had started early in the day and so did the fighting. Carl ran out of the house and jumped into the old Studebaker. He sat in the driveway revving it up. The kids ran for the house.

They all stood huddled together at the big front room window. Helen was still running towards the house.

He pinned little Helen against a tree. The revving of the car got louder as he held the break. He stopped just as she was hugging the tree. The bumper was pinned against her legs. She was screaming. Josey sent the boys to go get help.

Luckily Carl's dad came out and talked him into turning off the car.

Josey ran, grabbed Helen, took her into the house, and held her very tight. Josey, Helen, and the boys all cried and screamed in fear.

What evil could be in this man? Didn't God make everyone? He made him too, didn't he?

Another weekend came and without fail, more drinking and fighting went on.

Inez and Carl came in fighting and throwing things.

Inez threw splashes of Kerosene at Carl, trying to set him on fire. She took a big knife and slashed at him. She ran outside and sure enough he got in the damn car and hit her.

He carried her in the house and threw her on the bed. He kept kicking her with his steel toed boots. She went to the hospital with a fractured shoulder. They went on as usual, like nothing ever happened.

One Friday night, as expected, Inez and Carl came home after yet another night of heavy drinking. They were throwing dishes and furniture. The boys ran out the door. Carl thought that they were going to the neighbors to call the police.

They ran up the hill and into the back woods.

He grabbed his 22 automatic rifle and ran after the boys, shooting at them. They did not know how many shots were fired but, he emptied that gun on them. They ran up and down the hills until they reached the deep woods.

They hid until they thought maybe he passed out.

Before daylight the boys crept back into the house. Thank goodness, Carl and Inez were passed out.

Ray, Wayne, Gordon, Butch, and Clayton waited to see if he reacted when he woke up. As always he acted like nothing ever happened.

Chapter 20

One day while Josey was in junior high school, her cousin Sandy met her there.

Sandy sat down with Josey and asked her how things were at home. Josey told her everything. It seems that Sandy had left home to get away from the abuse. She knew Josey was telling her the truth. He had gotten too close to her a few times.

She took Josey to the welfare office. They talked with a social worker there.

The next day a social worker came to the house. They took Josey and Helen to live with their mother. Josey told her mother about the razor strap and everything else that they all endured while she was there.

One afternoon Josey came home from school and was met at the door. There was a fire at Inez and Carl's house. Everyone was alright but, Josey couldn't rest until she saw all of her brothers. There seemed to be a few house fires after that. The insurance companies wouldn't even insure them anymore.

Josey remembered seeing an insurance policy on Clayton and Gordon before she left home. She didn't understand why it was on the two youngest boys. She often wondered about that. She didn't quite know how insurance worked.

The boys did survive those fires but, there was one close call when they almost didn't get out. The other boys and Carl were gone. When the two boys got out of the house Inez was standing at the top of the hill screaming. The house went up in a big blaze. Nothing was left.

Years later Josey saw pictures that she was sure burned up in the house. The house was a big pile of ashes and nothing could have survived that.

As her mind went whirling back through all the memories, tears ran down her face. She couldn't stop remembering now. She did not want to remember anymore. "Please make the thoughts stop," she cried.

Josey remembered the day her mother had left them with their aunt and uncle. Inez and her mother were sisters. She remembered running down the road. "Don't leave us! Don't leave us! We will be good. We don't need food; we need you and nothing else!! Please! Please don't go!" She screamed as she fell to the ground crying for her mother. She was eight years old.

At that time Josey, her mother, Helen, and the boys lived in a little shack behind Carl's mother's house. It was an old goat house. There were cracks between the boards where daylight had shown through. Her mother couldn't find work with seven children to look after. There was very little food that was given to them.

Josey remembers eating onions and crackers. Clayton was just a baby and Helen a toddler when they lived there. They just had cow's milk most of the time. She didn't even care about that. She was glad to have her mother.

Aunt Inez and Uncle Carl came out of nowhere to visit and Josey wondered what the sudden visit was about. They lived a hundred and fifty miles away. To Josey that seemed a long ways away.

Her brothers and sister were out in the yard running and playing and they were told to stay outside. Josey was curious and wanted to know what was going on.

She heard her mother tell her sister that something needed to be done. "There was not enough food for all the kids. They are all losing weight and you can see their ribs. They need shoes and clothes and I cannot get any help," she said.

That is when they agreed to take all the children for a while. At least until she could provide a home, food, and clothing for them all. She signed custody papers for them and Inez agreed that it was only temporary. Inez had a job in a factory in St. Louis but agreed to move to the country. Carl could work on a farm where the house was included with the job.

They grabbed the few things that they had and settled into that house. Josey's mother Dorothy went to St. Louis looking for work. Inez soon got the call that their mother had cancer. Therefore, Dorothy went to stay with her and care for her. Josey loved her grandmother; she could always talk to her about anything.

Her grandmother was different than anyone else she knew. She could read fortune cards and Josey was fascinated by this.

Chapter 21

There was once when they all went to visit their grandmother. Josey remembers not wanting to go back to the farm then. Her Uncle Carl came in drunk that night falling down all over the house. Josey woke up to yelling and things slamming. Carl was leaning over her sick grandmother on the couch. She had gone blind with the cancer. She was yelling for help.

Dorothy came in to the living room and started screaming at Carl. "Get away from her you son-of-a-bitch. What in the hell are you doing to her? Leave her alone." Josey did not know what he was doing to her but, Josey knew that it was bad enough for her mother to be screaming and crying at him.

Inez woke up and of course yelled back at Dorothy. "We are taking the kids and leaving. You have no rights to them." Josey did not see her mother again until she went back to live with her. Even when the news came that her grandmother had passed away her Aunt Inez would not let her go to the funeral. She had to stay home and watch the other children. She hated her aunt for that and would never forgive her.

Josey very much remembered moving back in with her mother. Her mother took Inez and Carl to court several times but, it did no good. The abuse went on and no one knew. The courts would not listen and the children remained in the custody of Aunt Inez and Uncle Carl.

The weekend fighting continued and probably even got worse for the boys after the girls were taken.

Gordon left the house as the age of fourteen. He hitchhiked from state to state. Somehow he survived it.

Wayne ran away on April fool's day. Carl tried to barricade him in the kitchen but, he got out the back anyway. He ran across the yard looking back at Carl. He shouted, "April Fool's day Mother Fucker!"

The following weekend Carl and his brother fed Jim some alcohol until he passed out. They took him out and laid him on a set of train tracks. Thanks to God that no train came through those tracks that night.

He ran away the next day.

Ray and Clayton graduated and finally left home.

Inez died of Cancer.

Carl died in a house fire. He came home one night from the bar and fell asleep while he was cooking.

Josey was sad to hear about that. She didn't want to see him anymore after she left home but, she didn't want to hear about this happening to anyone. Not even him.

Chapter 22

Once again the birds sang and the grass grew green. The white cotton fields were bountiful. The gardens were full of big, bold melons and cucumbers were running wild. The tall green beans blew in the breeze and tomatoes were big and ripe.

All was good again.

Josey had two more sisters and three more brothers.

Her sister Virginia was a tiny little girl with long thick, red hair. She had freckles across her face.

Judy had beautiful wavy, blonde hair, like their mother.

Bobby was a baby when Josey was still at home. After she was married and left her mother, Rusty and Charley were born. Birth control was not an option for her and she was remarried.

Rusty and Charlie were both cute little boys with brownish blonde hair.

Finally all the children were grown up and on their own. They all remained very close.

Over the years Josey's father checked in and out of the crossbar hotel; otherwise known as the Missouri State Prison. He came to live with Josey and her family when he was older and was diagnosed with cancer. He died in her home where she took care of him.

Josey's mother, Dorothy eventually lived alone in their hometown in Missouri in a little house where her children visited her often. She died of heart failure in a St. Louis hospital with her children surrounding her.

Dorothy had a twin brother who had only lived a few months after they were born. She was a strong woman. She had a total of thirteen children with one that died of crib death. She named him David Eugene. She never got over his death; she had pictures of him in the bassinet that she kept in special places. She never talked about him.

Josey and her cousin Sandy were very close. She remembers when Sandy's first son was born at the house she lived in with Josey's mother. Sandy named him Brian. Josey remembers hearing the baby's first cries as she stood on the front yard that day. Sandy's son Blayne was born after Josey was married and moved to Michigan. Sandy died of Cancer.

As Josey sat on the porch going through her grocery ads trying to decide on dinner, she knew it wasn't going to be bean soup.

Her children came to the door asking if they could come out to play. Their rooms were all cleaned.

She asked them what they wanted for dinner and they all yelled out "fried chicken with biscuits and gravy." Josey just smiled and said "Ok! Go out and play with your friends, and have fun!"

That is exactly what they did.

Epilogue

Josey's brother Jim (Butch) came out of the army with an honorable discharge. He has five children.

Wayne retired from a big steel company, which he headed in St. Louis. He and his wife Dottie together had five children.

Raymond retired from the U.S. Navy and lives in California. He builds condos. He married the beautiful blonde Dana, who worked in a nearby hospital just like in the movies. They have one daughter.

Her brother Gordon doesn't roam anymore. He spent a short time in the crossbar hotel (jail). He is an Indian leader in a small community in Tennessee. He drives a cab and meets people from all walks of life. He has six children. His heart is at peace.

Clayton preaches the gospel. He often speaks at teen challenge. He spent a lot of time learning to believe in himself.

Little Helen passed away at the age forty-seven. She was a dedicated mother to her son and she was active in her church in St. Louis.

Her little sister Virginia lives in Missouri and has five sons along with her husband, who is a published writer.

Her sister Judy has six children together with her

husband. She is a seamstress and lives in Georgia.

Rusty works as a tree trimmer in Missouri and Michigan. He has four children.

Bobby works with wood burnings. He has a son and a daughter.

Josey's brother Charley is a jack of all traits. He can do just about anything. He has two daughters. he lives in New Mexico.

Josey loves all of her family. Every one of them!

She sometimes misses Missouri with the tall woods, the animals, the pink cotton flowers, the pink and white dogwood trees, the rolling foothills, the bountiful sunsets, and the roosters crowing into the daybreak. Every now and then she goes home to visit her family and her few friends. Josey and her sister-in-law Susie still visit some of the places they used to go like; the ice cream drive in, the place where the movie theater used to be, and the high school.

Josey always hoped to be someone of importance. Through experiences of her children and wisdom of life, she could have been a doctor or a lawyer.

She was a butcher, a baker, a soy candle maker, and even a construction worker.

And you know what! She finally broke into print.

Bev Beck Titles Include:

 01: Benny At The Bop™
ISBN: 9781590953747

 02: The Acorn Nuts™
ISBN: 9781590953754

 03: The Birthday Present™
ISBN: 9781590953761

 04: The Hollers Bunch Goes to Lunch™
ISBN: 9781590953778

 05: Can You Just Imagine™
ISBN: 9781590953785

 06: Hillbilly Heaven™
ISBN: 9781590954683

 07: The Curwood Acorns™
ISBN: 9781590951262

 08: Lonny Lemon™
ISBN: 9781648830143

09: Title: Josey's Hillbilly Heaven™

Author: Bev Beck
Publisher: TotalRecall Publications
Paper Back: ISBN: 9781648830921
eBook: ISBN: 9781648830938
Publication Date: 2021

Josey's Hillbilly Heaven is based on some truth, some fiction, with twist and turns to create some fun for her readers. Josey's experience growing up in the hills of Missouri helped set her standards and beliefs in her life and loves for a solid foundation of the person she is today.

Her book Hillbilly Heaven will let you know what a strong-willed youngster she was and the strong adult she is today.

www.ingramcontent.com/pod-product-compliance
Ingram Content Group UK Ltd.
Pitfield, Milton Keynes, MK11 3LW, UK
UKHW041949230426
12048UKWH00008B/220